D1081173

for Irene

MYRIAD BOOKS LIMITED
35 Bishopsthorpe Road, London SE26 4PA

First published in 2001 by
PICCADILLY PRESS LIMITED
5 Castle Road, London NW1 8PR
www.piccadillypress.co.uk

Text and illustrations copyright © Rachel Pank, 2001

Rachel Pank has asserted her right to be identified as the author and illustrator of this work in accordance with the Copyright, Designs and Patents Act, 1988.

All rights reserved. No part of this publication may be reproduced, stored in a retrieval system, or transmitted, in any form or by any means electronic, mechanical, photocopying or otherwise, without prior permission of the copyright owner.

ISBN 1 904736 61 0

Designed by Louise Millar

Printed in China

Rosie's Holiday

Rachel Pank

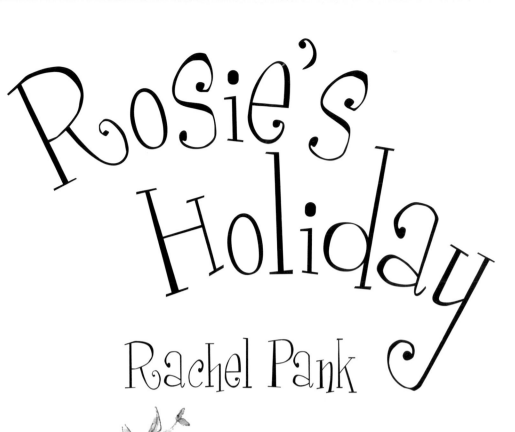

MYRIAD BOOKS LIMITED

"I don't **want** to go on holiday!"
said a very small girl in a very loud voice.

It was Rosie.

"I like my own room."

"I like my own garden."

"And . . . I like you **all**!" she bellowed
at the cats next door.

The following day, Dad packed the car,
but there wasn't room for everything.
Rosie could not take *all* her cuddly toys.

"Just **one**!" said Dad.

Her bike would not fit, or her duvet,
or the cats next door.

"**No!**" said Dad.
"We'll have to leave
those behind."

So Rosie hugged the cats.
"I will be back!"

She sat in the car wearing her holiday hat,
holding her holiday bag,
and wished she wasn't going.

When they got to their holiday home, Rosie saw the sea at the bottom of the garden. At first she pretended not to look, but then she saw big blue waves and boats!

Right next door there was a field of cows – with spots!
They chewed and smiled at Rosie. "Hello," she said.

Then Rosie followed Mum
and Dad inside.

She ran upstairs . . .

. . . and downstairs.

"My holiday bed
is bouncier than
my home bed!"
she shouted.

The next day they all went down to the beach.
Rosie filled her buckets with shells and pebbles.
"I might like it here," she told baby Toby.

Rosie loved the sea.

Every day
she splished . . .

and splashed . . .

and sploshed!

On the last night of the holiday, Rosie stayed up late. She watched hundreds of twinkling, sparkling stars in the night sky.

"I **do** like it here," she whispered to her mum and dad.

In the morning, Rosie visited
all her favourite places.
"I want to take the
cows home!" she said.

"They like it here," said Dad.
"This is where they belong."
The cows blinked their eyes
and said their goodbyes.

"I want to take the sand and the sea home," Rosie sniffed. "Look," said Mum. "Here are all your shells and pebbles to take back. And I've made you this necklace. Now we have to pack and get ready to go."

"I DON'T WANT TO GO HOME!" cried Rosie.

But as soon as they got back to her *very own* home,
Rosie raced into the garden.
"You forgot your shells!" called Dad.

But Rosie couldn't wait.

"HELLO!" she shouted to her garden, her
paddling pool, the stars and the sky. She hugged
her big crocodile and jumped on to her bike.

"It's ME!" she yelled to the cats over the fence . . .

"I'm back!"